HOG-EYE

Susan Meddaugh

Houghton Mifflin Company Boston

1 9 9 5

To Walter
and the Maple Street bus riders

Walter Lorraine (wл) Books

Library of Congress Cataloging-in-Publication Data

Meddaugh, Susan.
  Hog eye / written and illustrated by Susan Meddaugh.
  p.   cm.
  Summary: A young pig uses her ability to read to outwit a wolf
that intends to eat her.
  ISBN 0-395-74276-5
  [1. Pigs—Fiction.   2. Wolves—Fiction.   3. Reading—Fiction.
4. Poison ivy—Fiction.]   I. Title.
PZ7.M51273Ho   1995   95-3951
[E]—dc20   CIP
                 AC

Printed in the United States of America
10 9 8 7 6 5 4 3 2 1

Yesterday my whole family met me at the door. They wanted to know why I didn't go to school. So I told them the true story.

It's not MY fault. It's . . .

SCHOOL BUS 37. The kids are terrible, and my big
brother, who is supposed to help me, is the worst one of all.
I wish I had a magic spell to make them all disappear!

I don't like school bus 37.
So yesterday I took my time getting to the corner . . .

. . . and when I got on the bus, there were no other kids.
"My wish came true!" I thought.

Then I realized I was on the wrong bus.

You weren't paying attention.

At first I was just a little worried.

"Maybe this bus is going a different way to school," I thought. But the bus drove right past the school, and soon it was getting farther and farther away from anything I recognized.

So I went to the bus driver and calmly told him that I wanted to get off.

The bus driver let me off at the side of the road. I had
no idea where I was.

Fortunately there was a sign, and you know I'm a good reader. If I followed the road, it would take a long time to get home. But if I followed the path through the forest, I could be home before dark.

How many times have we told you: Never go in the forest alone!

Many many times!

I decided to take the path.

No sooner had I entered the forest when a wolf grabbed
me and threw me into a sack.

I was scared but cool.

When we got to his terrible, gloomy cave, the wolf took
a big pot and put it on the stove. He was singing a song
about soup.

Stalling for time, I said, "That is not how MY mommy
makes soup. She GOES OUT and gets LOTS of fresh
ingredients, and her soup is the best."

"Is not!" said the wolf. "MY mommy made the best soup!
I'll just get her cookbook and you'll see!"
The wolf grabbed a book from a dusty shelf.

"There," he said. "You find my mommy's recipe for soup
and read it to me."

Our daughter is helping a wolf make soup...

That was when I realized something very interesting.

"It's too bad you can't read," I said.
"Of course I can read!" snapped the wolf. "I just don't want to read today. You read."

So I said, "The first ingredients are . . . carrots and potatoes
. . . from Mr. Gray's garden."

The wolf tied me to a table leg and ran off to find Mr.
Gray's garden.

Did you tell him about the traps?

This was my chance. While he was gone, I tried to untie
the rope.
But the knot was too tight, and soon the wolf was back.
"What's next?" he asked crankily.

"Sweet onions," I told him, ". . . and green peppers from
the foot of . . .

Devil's Cliff."

As soon as he left, I tried to chew through the rope, but again the wolf returned before I could escape.

So I gave him another ingredient:
"Pure water from Torrential Falls."

The wolf limped off with a bucket.

I was working on my third escape plan when the wolf
staggered through the door with the bucket of water.
"Enough!" he gasped. "I'm hungry."

I said to the wolf, "There is only one more ingredient, but it's the most important ingredient of all. Without this ingredient, the soup will taste like spit."

I drew the wolf a picture so he would be sure to get the right plant.
"This is Green Threeleaf."

I gave the wolf precise instructions:
"Find a large patch of it, because the more you get, the better the soup.

"Crush the leaves. The easiest way to do this is to roll around in them.

"Gather the juiciest leaves and vines and put them inside your shirt to keep them warm."

The wolf did exactly as he was told.

But when he got back, he said, "TIME TO MAKE THE SOUP!"
I could tell he meant it.

That was when I cast my magic spell on him.
"Wolf," I said "You have just brought me the final
ingredient for my magic potion. Prepare to feel the power
of HOG-EYE!"

"Hoo ha!" laughed the wolf. "That's a good one."
He picked up a match.

I opened my eyes as wide as I could and fixed him with a
mighty stare.
"Careful—if you light that match,
you will have the urge to scratch."

The wolf lit the match.
"Hog-eye! Hog-eye! Magic stare!
Make him itchy everywhere.
On his nose and in his hair.
Even in his underwear!"

At first nothing happened.
The wolf lit a fire under the pot. He put the carrots,
onions, green peppers, and potatoes into the pot. He was
reaching for me when . . .

. . . he stopped to scratch

one

tiny

little

itch.

One scratch led to another.

And another.

The more he scratched,

the more he itched,

and the more he itched,

the more he scratched . . .

until finally he cried.

STOP the HOG-EYE!
I'll do anything you ask...

I told him I would release the spell after he let me go.

And, I demanded a nice apology!

PIGGI BORO

"Hmmm," said my father.
"Ahhhh," said my mother.
My brother said, "I feel itchy."

Today I beat my brother to the corner.